Carrie
the Snow Cap
Fairy

Special thanks to Narinder Dhami

ISBN 978-0-545-60530-4

Previously published as Green Fairies #7: *Carrie the Snow Cap Fairy* by Orchard U.K. in 2009.

12 11 10 9 8 7 6 5 4 3 2 1 14 15 16 17 18 19/0

Printed in the U.S.A. 40

This edition first printing, July 2014

Carrie the Snow Cap Fairy

by Daisy Meadows

SCHOLASTIC INC.

The Fairyland Palace
River Rapids
Seabury
Ferry
Rain Forest

Jack Frost's
Ice Castle
Rainspell Island
Wildlife
Garden
Lake
Vacation Cottage
Harbor
Beach
Coral
Reef
Ice Cap

The Earth Fairies must be dreaming
If they think they can escape my scheming.
My goblins are by far the greenest,
And I am definitely the meanest.

Seven fairies out to save the earth?
This very idea fills me with mirth!
I'm sure the world has had enough
Of fairy magic and all that stuff.

So I'm going to steal the fairies' wands
And send them into human lands.
The fairies will think all is lost,
Defeated again—by me, Jack Frost!

Contents

Frosty Leaves

"Brrr!" Shivering, Rachel Walker glanced across the bedroom at her best friend. Kirsty Tate was just waking up, too. "It's really cold this morning, isn't it?"

Kirsty yawned and nodded. "It's freezing," she agreed. "It's been getting colder all week."

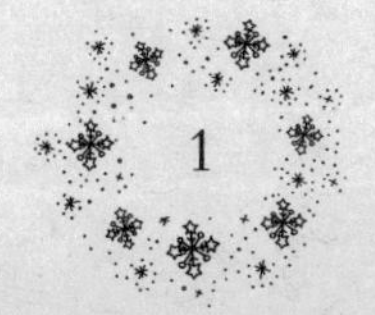

"Well, I suppose it *is* getting late in the year," said Rachel. She sat up in bed, wrapping the comforter around her shoulders. "It'll be winter soon— but I didn't expect the weather to change quite so fast!"

"Haven't we had a wonderful vacation though, Rachel?" Kirsty sighed happily. "It's been so special to come back to Rainspell Island, where we first met."

The Walkers and the Tates were spending the fall break together in a pretty little cottage on beautiful, magical Rainspell Island.

"Yes, it's been fabulous!" Rachel

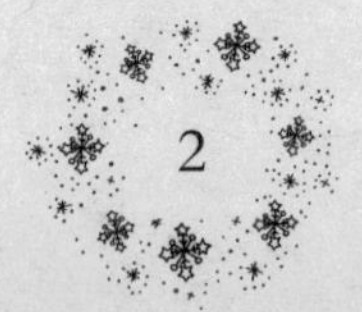

smiled. "And we're even having another fairy adventure, just like the first time we visited Rainspell."

"Only this time it was *our* turn to ask the fairies for help," Kirsty pointed out.

When Kirsty and Rachel had returned to Rainspell Island a week ago, they'd been horrified to see the wide, golden beach covered in litter. So they'd asked the king and queen of Fairyland if their fairy friends could help them clean up the human environment.

The king and queen had explained to the girls that fairy magic could only do so much, and that humans had to help

the environment, too. But they had agreed that the seven fairies who were about to complete their training could become the Earth Fairies for a trial period. They would work together with Rachel and Kirsty to try to make the world a cleaner place. If the fairies completed their training successfully, protecting the environment would become their permanent task.

But just as the Earth Fairies were about to be presented with their new wands, Jack Frost and his goblins had zoomed toward them on an ice bolt. The goblins had snatched all seven wands, and then Jack Frost's icy magic had sent them tumbling into the human world.

Jack Frost had declared that the world didn't need any more fairies flitting

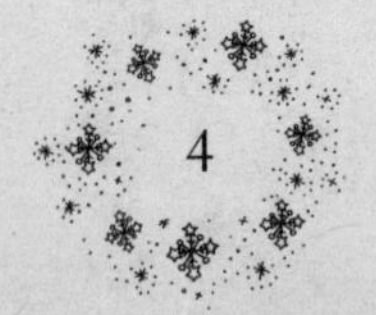

around doing good deeds. Rachel and Kirsty had promised the king and queen that they would do their best to get all the wands safely back into the hands of the Earth Fairies.

"Wasn't it *just* like Jack Frost and his goblins to steal all the wands?" Kirsty said, shuddering at the memory. "Thank goodness we've been able to find six of them, Rachel."

"Yes, with the help of Nicole, Isabella, Edie, Coral, Lily, and Milly," Rachel replied. "But we still have to find Carrie the Snow Cap Fairy's wand."

Kirsty looked worried. "If we don't

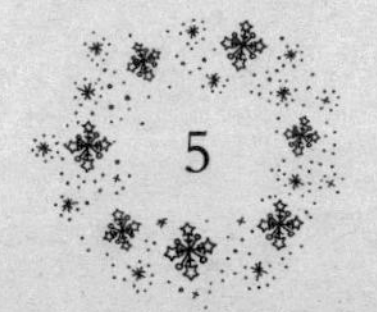

find Carrie's wand, the fairies will fail their final exam, and then they won't be able to keep helping the environment."

"But you know what Queen Titania always says," Rachel reminded Kirsty as she went over to open the curtains. "We have to wait for the magic to come to *us*."

"I know," Kirsty said with a sigh. "But we don't have much time—we're going home later today."

As Rachel opened the curtains wide, she gave a surprised gasp. "Kirsty, come and look!"

Kirsty ran to join Rachel at the window. There had been a heavy frost during the night, and the trees, flowers, and grass in the cottage garden were covered with a thin layer of white ice that glittered in the morning sunshine.

"Doesn't the garden look beautiful?" Kirsty exclaimed.

"Let's go out before it all melts," Rachel suggested.

The girls dressed quickly and ran downstairs. The front door of the cottage

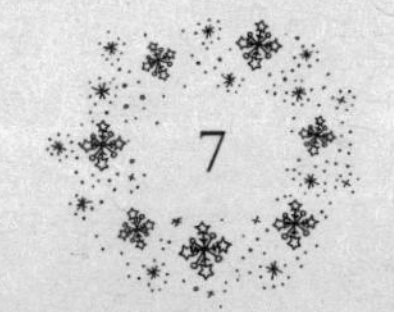

was open. Mr. Walker had just begun sprinkling sand on the path to make the ice less slippery.

"Morning, girls," he said as Rachel and Kirsty stepped outside. "Be careful you don't slip."

"We won't," Rachel replied. But as she spoke, her foot slid away from her, and Kirsty had to grab her arm to keep her from falling over.

Rachel's

dad grinned. "See what I mean?"

"Why do you think it got so cold all of a sudden, Mr. Walker?" Kirsty asked.

"I suppose it's because of climate change," Mr. Walker replied, scattering a handful of sand across the path. "Climate change can cause some strange weather—too cold, too hot, too wet. Overall though, the world is getting hotter. Even the polar ice caps are melting," Mr. Walker explained. "That's very bad news for the world because it means in years to come the seas will rise, and then there will likely be more floods." He emptied

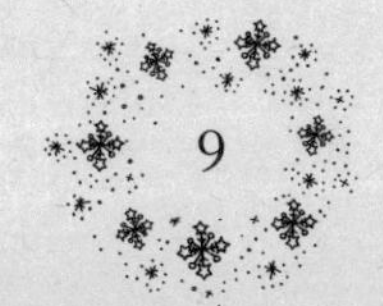

out the last grains of sand, then glanced at his watch. "I need to go help with the packing. We're leaving soon."

Rachel turned to Kirsty as Mr. Walker hurried into the house.

"We *have to* find Carrie's wand before we leave Rainspell Island," Rachel whispered. "We need her help to fight climate change!"

"We'll just have to keep our eyes open," replied Kirsty,

glancing around. "The garden looks so pretty, doesn't it, Rachel? The frost is making everything sparkle in the sunshine."

"Look at the frosty leaves on that plant." Rachel pointed toward the back of the garden. "They seem to be almost glowing!"

The girls went to take a look. As they got closer, they could see something fluttering around the leaves. At first, they thought it was a

butterfly. But then Kirsty grabbed Rachel's arm, her face full of excitement.

"I can see a fairy!" Kirsty cried. The fairy was dressed in a green fake-fur jacket over a cozy wool sweater. She wore mittens, and dark blue jeans tucked into furry boots. She was hovering above a frosty leaf. As Rachel and Kirsty watched, the fairy gently kissed the leaf's surface. Instantly, the frost melted away, and the leaf glowed a bright green.

At once, the fairy spotted Rachel and Kirsty and waved.

"Girls!" she called. "Do you remember me? I'm Carrie the Snow Cap Fairy!"

Goblins on Ice

"Of course we remember you, Carrie!" Rachel said.

"We're so happy to see you," Kirsty added with a smile.

"And I'm thrilled to see *you*," declared Carrie, zooming over to them. "Girls, I desperately need my wand back! The polar ice caps are melting, and I *have* to try to keep that from happening."

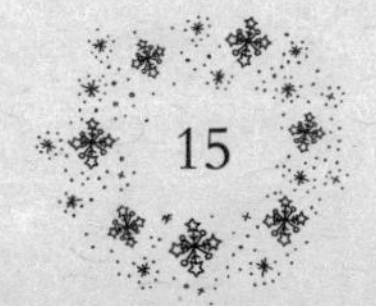

"Do you have any idea where your wand is?" asked Rachel.

Carrie nodded. "Oh, yes," she replied. "But it's far away from here, in the South Pole—with the goblins!" She frowned. "You know that my magic is limited without my wand because I'm still a fairy-in-training. So I'll have to use what little magic I have to get there."

"Can we still come with you?" Kirsty asked hopefully.

Rachel nodded. "We want to help."

Carrie sighed with relief. "I was hoping you would. Let's go, girls!" she cried. "There's no time to lose."

Carrie fluttered above Rachel and Kirsty, waving her hand. A shower of magic fairy dust floated down around the girls. As it did, the frosty garden began to shimmer and sparkle even more brightly in the sunshine. Rachel and Kirsty were so dazzled, they had to close their eyes. The next moment they felt themselves being whisked off their feet, and then they were flying through the air.

"We've arrived, girls!" Carrie cried joyfully. "I've made sure you're going to be nice and cozy here in my cold but beautiful South Pole!"

The girls eagerly opened their eyes. Carrie had turned them into fairies with her magic, and they were hovering high up in the air. They were now wearing fluffy white earmuffs, mittens, furry boots, and shimmering silver parkas. And there were glittering fairy wings on their shoulders!

Freezing cold air swirled around

Rachel and Kirsty as they looked down at the landscape below them. The girls were utterly amazed by what they saw.

They were floating above vast, icy plains that stretched in every direction, as far as the eye could see. The plains were bordered by an enormous ocean. The greenish-blue water was covered with huge, towering icebergs and thick flat sheets of ice that moved slowly across the surface.

In the distance the girls could see snow-

covered mountains, their peaks glistening in the pale light of the sun.

"This is so beautiful!" Kirsty gasped. "But there are hardly any plants or trees!"

"That's because the ice never really melts very much, even in summer," Carrie explained. "At certain times of the year, the whole ocean freezes over!"

Suddenly, a seal popped his sleek head out of the icy water. He stared curiously up at Carrie and the girls with shiny, dark eyes. Then, with one swift flick of his tail, he disappeared again.

"Will we see any polar bears?" Rachel asked, looking around eagerly.

Carrie laughed. "Animals like polar bears and walruses and caribou live in the *North* Pole!" she told the girls. "But there are lots of different animals here. I'll show you around while we search for my wand. Come on!"

Rachel and Kirsty quickly flew after Carrie as she jetted over the water.

"Look at the icebergs below us," Kirsty said to Rachel. "They're the most amazing shapes!"

"And so big," Rachel added. "They

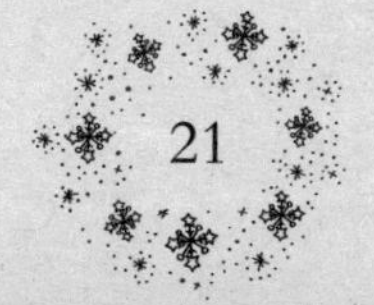

look taller than our cottage back on Rainspell!"

Just then a spray of sea water shot into the air. Carrie and the girls had to dodge it to avoid getting splashed.

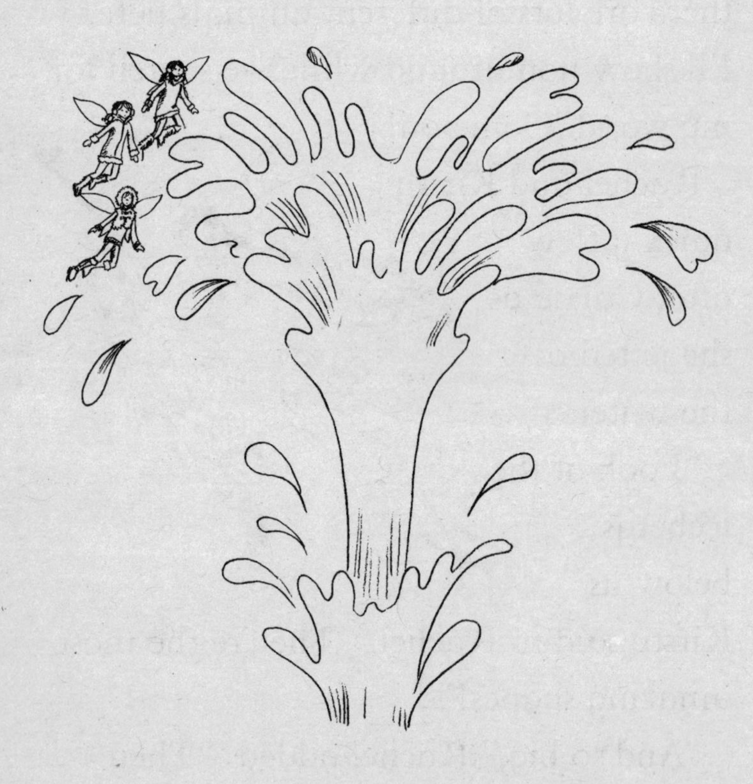

"See the blue whale, girls?" Carrie yelled. "That water came from his blowhole!"

Rachel and Kirsty glanced down and just caught a glimpse of the enormous whale as he dove underwater again.

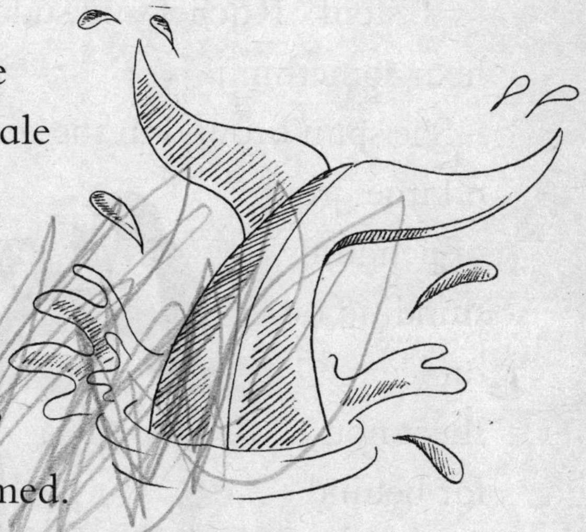

"There's so much to see!" Kirsty exclaimed. It was then that she spotted something glinting in the sunshine just ahead of them.

"Oh! What's *that*?" Kirsty cried, pointing it out to Rachel and Carrie.

When the three friends flew closer,

they saw that it was a long, thin icicle hanging from an iceberg.

Kirsty's face fell. "I thought it was the wand." She sighed.

"Listen!" Rachel said suddenly. "I can hear something!"

She spun around in the air and spotted a large group of penguins standing on an ice sheet not far behind them. The penguins were squawking and seemed very annoyed.

"Let's go and check it out," Carrie suggested.

They flew toward the penguins, but as they got closer, Kirsty gasped. "Goblins!" she cried.

Three goblins were standing on the sheet of ice, surrounded by penguins. They were all arguing loudly.

"I wonder what they're fighting about," Carrie said, puzzled. But Kirsty had already spotted something.

"See the big penguin at the front?" Kirsty pointed out, breathless with

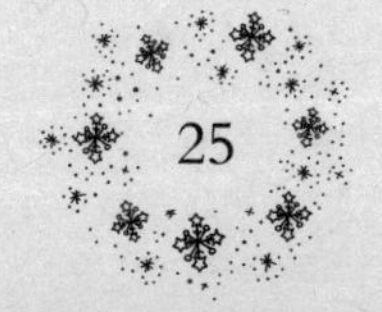

excitement. "He has your wand, Carrie!"

The penguin was holding the gleaming wand firmly between his black flippers. When one of the goblins lunged to grab it, the other penguins immediately rushed forward, flapping their flippers at the goblin. He quickly retreated, scowling.

"The penguins don't want to give up the wand!" Rachel said with a grin.

The three goblins were muttering among themselves. Suddenly, they all dashed toward the big penguin.

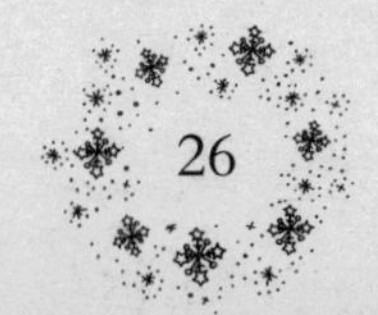

They took him by surprise, and one of the goblins managed to grab the end of the wand. But the big penguin, squawking with rage, held tightly on to the other end.

"They're playing tug-of-war!" Kirsty laughed as the other penguins and goblins rushed to join the battle for the wand.

The goblins were outnumbered by the penguins, but they were determined not to give in. They jumped up and down, tugging hard at the wand.

Suddenly, there was a loud CRACK!

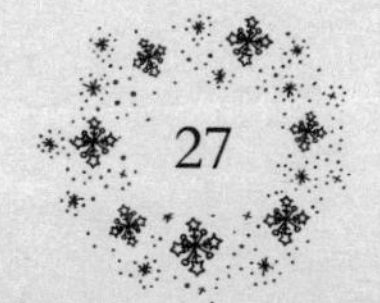

"What's that?" Kirsty gasped.

"The sheet of ice has cracked in two!" Carrie shouted.

The ice that the goblins and penguins were standing on had broken away from the main sheet and was floating away. The goblins were thrown off-balance, but the smallest one just managed to wrestle the wand from the big penguin as he fell over.

"I got it!" the goblin roared triumphantly, waving the wand in the air.

"Give it to *me*!" the others yelled, both trying to grab it.

Looking disgusted with the goblins, the penguins dove into the water and swam off. Meanwhile, the piece of ice continued to float away as the goblins argued over the wand.

"The goblins don't realize it, but they're stranded and floating out to sea!" Rachel exclaimed.

"Yes, they're in great danger," Carrie added anxiously. "And they're taking my wand with them!"

Jack Frost Appears

Carrie, Rachel, and Kirsty immediately flew over to the goblins.

"You're in big trouble!" Carrie called down to them. "You're floating right out to sea, and what will you do then?"

The goblins stopped arguing. They looked around and realized that Carrie was right. Panic spread across their faces.

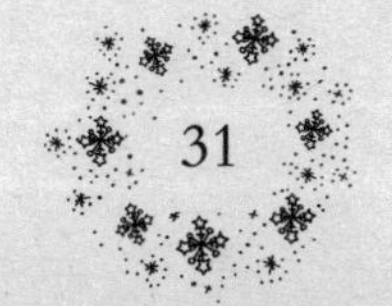

"HELP!" they shouted loudly.

"Give us the wand, and we'll make sure you get safely back to the shore," Kirsty offered.

The goblins stared suspiciously up at the three friends. Then they made a huddle and began muttering to one another.

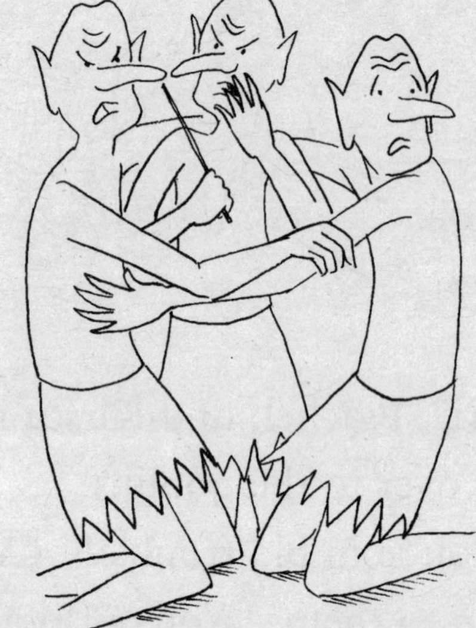

"We don't need the help of any silly fairies!" the biggest goblin grumbled. "Jack Frost is coming very soon to get the wand."

"Yes, he loves all this ice and snow,"

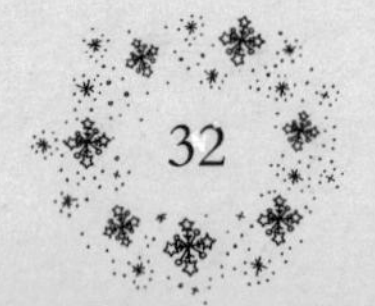

the smallest goblin chimed in, waving the wand around. "And he can't *wait* to have another wand for winter."

"Jack Frost must be on his way by now," said the third goblin. "*He'll* help us! So there!" And he rudely poked his tongue out at Carrie and the girls.

"We have to get the wand back before Jack Frost arrives," Carrie whispered urgently to Rachel and Kirsty.

"Let's fly down and try to grab it," Rachel suggested.

But as the three friends flew lower, the smallest goblin pointed the wand at them

like a warning. "Keep away!" he shouted. "Or I'll use my magic to stop you!"

"Don't do that!" Carrie warned him. "The magic is very unpredictable in the wrong hands—"

But the goblins weren't listening. The biggest goblin lunged forward and grabbed the wand from the other one. Then he began waving it wildly in the air, chanting a silly spell:

"We love ice,
We love snow,
Do we love fairies?
No, no, NO!
We want snowballs,
Not to play,
So we can shoo
These fairies away!"

Carrie and the girls watched anxiously as a few sparkles of fairy dust drifted from the wand. Suddenly an enormous snowball fell from the sky and landed with a SPLAT right on top of the goblins. They disappeared into the giant pile of snow, and all Carrie and the girls could see were their legs sticking out. The three friends couldn't help laughing as the silly goblins wiggled their way out of the snow and then shook themselves off.

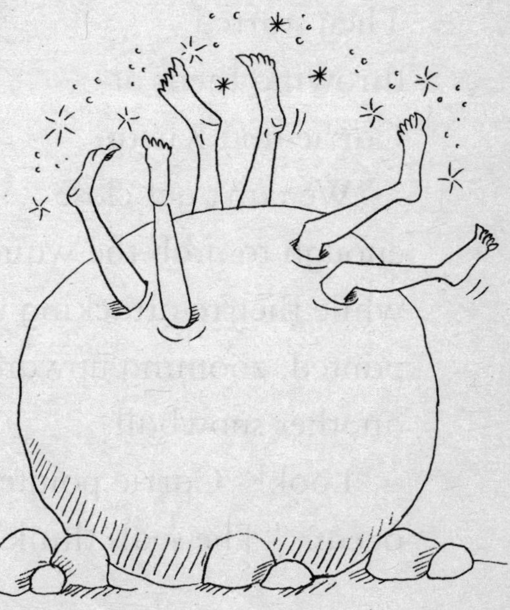

"Get them!" the smallest goblin yelled. Quickly, he rolled some snow into a snowball and hurled it right at Rachel. She ducked, but now the other two goblins were making snowballs, too. They started throwing them at Carrie and Kirsty.

"We can't get close enough to grab the wand while they're attacking us!" Kirsty panted, zooming upward to avoid another snowball.

"Look!" Carrie pointed down at the ocean. "The seals think this is a game!"

The girls glanced down and saw several seals bobbing around in the water. As the snowballs flew, the seals batted them with their flippers. They honked with delight whenever they hit one.

Suddenly, Rachel noticed a tall, thin, spiky figure standing on the icy shore.

"Oh, no!" she whispered to Carrie and Kirsty. "It's Jack Frost!"

The goblins had not noticed that Jack Frost had arrived. The biggest one threw a snowball at Carrie, but he slipped slightly as he threw it. Instead of hitting the fairy, the snowball zoomed toward the shore. It hit Jack Frost smack in the face. Carrie, Rachel, and Kirsty grinned at each other.

"STOP!" Jack Frost roared furiously, wiping the snow away.

"Oh, no!" the biggest goblin muttered, looking horrified.

“We knew you’d come to rescue us,” the smallest goblin called to Jack Frost.

Jack Frost scowled. “I should let you float right out to sea!” he snapped.

“Sorry! Sorry!” muttered the biggest goblin. “But look, we have the wand—you should be proud of us!” He waved it in the air.

“How are we going to get the wand back *now*?” Kirsty whispered in dismay as Jack Frost smiled smugly.

"We'll have to try to persuade him to give my wand back!" Carrie said in a determined voice.

She flew closer to Jack Frost, with Rachel and Kirsty right behind her.

"Actually, that wand belongs to Carrie," Kirsty called to Jack Frost.

"And one way or another, we have to get it back," Rachel added bravely. "It's really important for the environment."

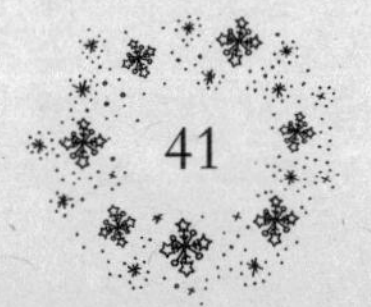

Jack Frost burst out laughing. "More silly fairies who do good deeds!" he jeered. Then he raised his wand and sent a glittering stream of frosty sparkles shooting toward the sea. As the sparkles flew through the air, they formed a bridge from the shore to the ice sheet where the goblins stood. The goblins whooped and cheered.

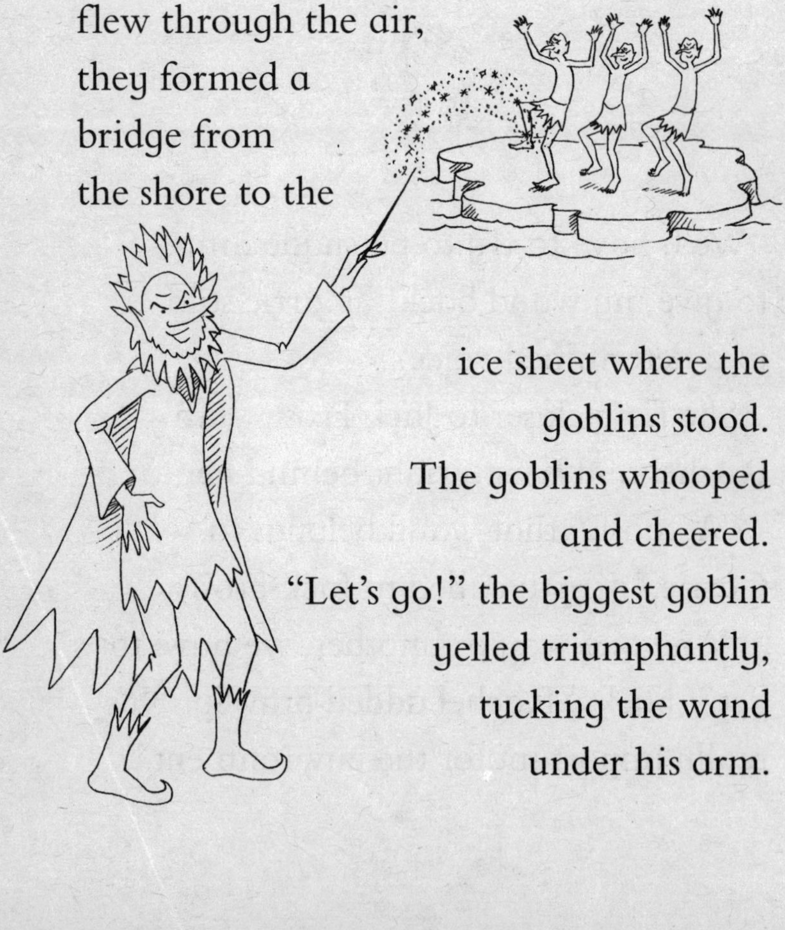

"Let's go!" the biggest goblin yelled triumphantly, tucking the wand under his arm.

"*I* should give the wand to Jack Frost," the smallest goblin said, scowling at him, "because *I* was the one who got it back from the penguins."

"No way!" the biggest goblin declared.

"Well, I haven't even had a turn at holding the wand yet!" the third goblin complained, trying to grab it from the biggest goblin.

The goblins began fighting over the wand, until the smallest goblin slipped on the ice.

"Help!" he shouted as he toppled head-first into the freezing ocean.

Meanwhile, the third goblin had managed to grab the wand, and now he rushed across the ice bridge toward Jack Frost. He ignored the goblin in the water, and so did the biggest goblin, who dashed after him, shrieking with rage.

"We'd better help him, girls," Carrie said quickly.

The three friends flew down to the goblin who was splashing and spluttering in the cold water. A group of seals had surrounded him, stopping him from floating farther out to sea. Summoning all of her magic, Carrie managed to push the goblin out of the water and

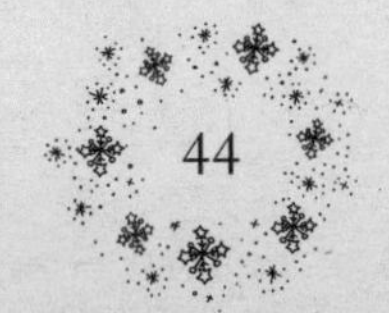

back onto the icy shore. He stood, dripping and shivering, next to Jack Frost and the other goblins.

"I'm grateful to you for helping my goblin helper," Jack Frost called out. "But I still won't give you the wand!"

"Be careful, girls!" Carrie gasped as Jack Frost raised his own wand. "He's going to shoot an ice bolt at us!"

There was a flash of chilly white as the ice bolt flew from Jack Frost's wand. But, to everyone's amazement, it just fell to

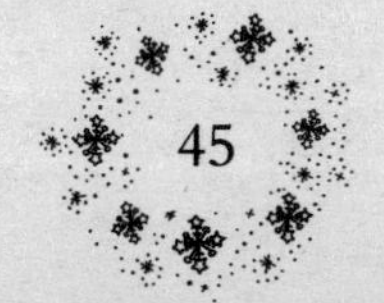

the ground. The bolt landed at Jack Frost's feet with a thud, instead of zipping through the air like his ice bolts usually did.

Frowning, Jack Frost tried again. This time the ice bolt melted and turned to slushy water in midair.

"Look!" the biggest goblin yelled. "The ice bridge is melting, too!"

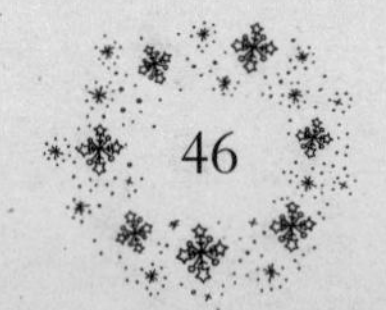

Jack Frost glared up at Carrie, Rachel, and Kirsty, who were hovering a short distance away. "What kind of magic are you using against my icy powers?" he raged.

"We're not using any magic," Carrie replied. "It's climate change!"

"The temperature of the earth is rising," explained Rachel.

"So the warmer air must be affecting your icy powers," Kirsty pointed out.

"Does this mean I might lose my ice magic?" Jack Frost asked in horror.

Rachel nodded. "If Carrie doesn't get her wand back, there'll be no Earth Fairies, and that will be terrible for the environment," she said. "Then you'll just be plain old Jack, instead of Jack Frost!"

Jack Frost was silent for a moment.

"Very well," he muttered at last. "I'll give you your wand back." He held it out to Carrie.

Looking relieved, Carrie swooped down to take the wand. But at the last moment Jack Frost changed his mind and snatched it away. Carrie tried again, but once again Jack Frost held on to the wand tightly.

"I promise to do my very best to keep the snow and ice caps cold if you'll give me my wand back," Carrie said earnestly. "But you and your goblins have to help, too. For

instance, you shouldn't be wasting energy."

"Maybe you could turn off the lights in your Ice Castle when you're not using them," Kirsty suggested.

"And you could start recycling," added Rachel. "Maybe you could transform your magic powers into some kind of icy energy that you could use for power in the castle?"

Jack Frost frowned thoughtfully. Carrie, Kirsty, and Rachel held their breath.

"Well," Jack Frost said with a sigh, "I'll try to think of something. But only because I love the cold, and I can't bear to see my Ice Castle melt. It has nothing to do with helping you pesky fairies!"

Then he handed the wand reluctantly to Carrie.

The moment Carrie touched her wand, a sparkling icy breeze sprang up around the three friends and whisked them off to Fairyland in the blink of an eye.

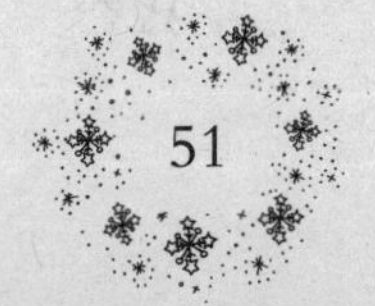

A few seconds later they landed in the palace gardens. Rachel and Kirsty smiled when they saw the king and queen and Bertram, the frog footman, waiting for them.

"Welcome back, Carrie, Rachel, and Kirsty!" the queen called.

"All of the Earth Fairies have now passed their final exam," the king announced. "Good job! May I have your wand, please, Carrie?"

Rachel and Kirsty beamed as Carrie handed her wand to the king. He in turn gave the wand to Bertram, who hopped away with it.

"We'll return all the wands when they're full of Fairyland magic," the king explained with a smile. "Now, let's join the other Earth Fairies at the Seeing Pool."

They all made their way through the colorful palace gardens toward the golden Seeing Pool. Nicole, Isabella, Edie, Coral, Lily, and Milly waved excitedly at Rachel, Kirsty, and Carrie as they joined them. They all chatted with excitement about their amazing adventures.

After a while, the queen addressed them. "You've made everyone in Fairyland very

proud," she declared. "And now here comes Bertram. Your wands have been powered up, and it's time for the Fairyland Wand Ceremony!"

Bertram hopped forward, carrying a tray with seven wands. Rachel and Kirsty could see that the wands now glowed with the brightness of the full moon.

As the queen handed Nicole the Beach Fairy her new wand, a rainbow of sparkles burst from it. Rachel and Kirsty gasped with delight as the sparkles zoomed up into the sky and floated there on the breeze. This happened six more times as the other six fairies were presented with their wands. Then all the sparkles formed themselves into a glittering, luminous rainbow, high in the sky above Fairyland.

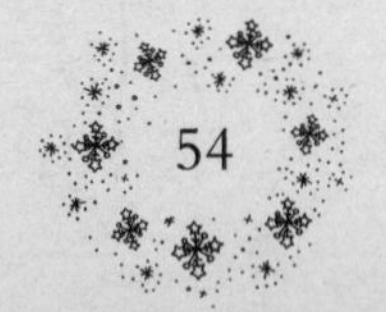

"Congratulations!" the queen told the Earth Fairies, as Rachel and Kirsty applauded. "You've all done very well, but there's more work to do."

Smiling, the seven fairies fluttered up into the air, waving at Rachel, Kirsty, and the king and queen. Then they zipped away in seven different directions, heading into the human world to their special environments.

"Thank you, girls, for coming up with the idea for the Earth Fairies," the king said. "But their work is only just beginning!"

"Yes," the queen agreed. "The world has many environmental problems, and fairies alone will never be able to solve them all. We need human help!"

"We'll keep doing our best," Rachel promised. But Kirsty was frowning. "But will it be enough?" she asked sadly. "There's so much to do! There's polluted air, the melting

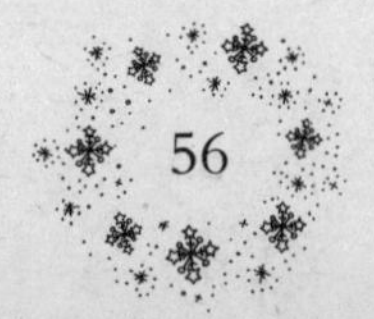

ice caps, the damaged coral reefs, the trash on the beaches and in the rivers and the parks, and the destruction of the rain forest."

"What can two girls and seven fairies *really* do to save the planet?" Rachel sighed.

The queen put her arms around the girls. "Every person's effort makes a difference!" she told them. "If you each get some of your friends to do their part to help the environment, and then those friends tell some more friends and so on . . . just imagine what a big impact that will make. And it will all start with two smart young girls like *you*!"

Rachel and Kirsty looked at each other, both feeling a rush of pride. Then the king beckoned Bertram to come forward. On the wand tray were two little green bags the girls hadn't noticed before. The queen handed one of the bags to Rachel and one to Kirsty.

"Take a look inside," the queen said with a smile.

Curiously, the girls peeked inside the bags. Inside were some small golden seeds.

"They're magic seeds," the king explained. "If you plant them and care for them, they'll grow into big strong trees, a memory of your adventures with the Earth Fairies!"

"We'll plant them as soon as we get home," Kirsty promised.

"And they'll remind us that we need to look after the Earth!" added Rachel.

"Thank you again, girls," the queen said, lifting her wand. "Now it's time to send you home!"

As a mist of fairy dust swirled around the girls, they waved good-bye to their Fairyland friends. Just a few seconds later, Rachel and Kirsty found themselves back in the garden of their cottage. The sun was now shining brightly, and almost all the frost had melted.

"Oh, there you are!" said Mr. Walker, staggering out of the front door with two heavy suitcases. "We're ready to leave."

Rachel's mom and Kirsty's parents followed him out of the cottage.

"Hasn't it been a wonderful trip, girls?" Kirsty's dad said with a smile.

Kirsty and Rachel nodded eagerly.

"And now we have lots of ideas about

how we can help the environment!" Kirsty replied. "We're going to pick up litter, and recycle more stuff, and make a difference, wherever we can."

"We're going to try to save energy by turning off lights," Rachel added. "And can we walk more and take public transportation instead of using the car sometimes? We're also going to ask our teachers if we can learn more about the environment and hold fund-raising events, and all kinds of other things!"

"That's very impressive, girls!" Mrs. Tate smiled. "But why have you suddenly become so interested in the environment?"

Rachel and Kirsty glanced knowingly at each other.

"Oh, we met some people here on Rainspell who've shown us the importance of taking care of our planet," Rachel explained.

"That's great!" said Mrs. Walker. "We'll help you all we can."

The girls shared a secret smile. What

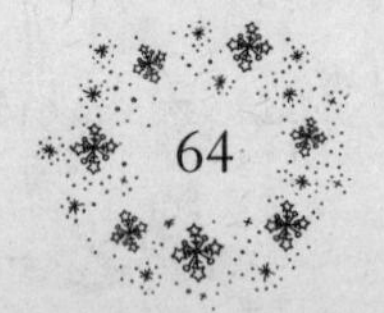

an amazing week it had been!

"It's a shame we have to say good-bye, Rachel," Kirsty said with a sigh. "But we'll see each other again soon, won't we?"

Rachel nodded. "Of course we will," she exclaimed. "After all, we're going to have lots more wonderful adventures with our magical fairy friends!"

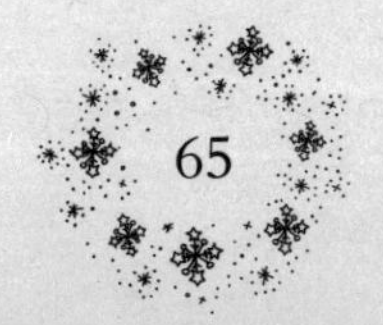

SPECIAL EDITION

Don't miss any of Rachel and Kirsty's other fairy adventures! Check out this magical sneak peek of

Natalie the Christmas Stocking Fairy!

Butter and Bother

"I love making pies at Christmastime," said Rachel Walker, sifting flour and salt into a heavy mixing bowl.

"Me, too," said her best friend, Kirsty Tate, opening a jar of cinnamon and taking a deep sniff. "The ingredients have such a Christmassy, spicy smell!"

"What does the recipe say next?" asked Rachel as Kirsty washed her hands.

Kirsty turned the page of the cookbook that was propped up on the kitchen counter.

"Rub the butter in with your fingers until the mixture looks like fine crumbs," she read.

Rachel opened the fridge and then frowned.

"Kirsty, did you already take the butter out of the fridge?"

"No," said Kirsty in surprise.

"That's funny," said Rachel. "I was sure we had some."

"Maybe we put it somewhere else," Kirsty suggested. "Let's look around."

They searched high and low, but the butter was nowhere to be found.

Just then, Mr. Tate walked into the kitchen, looking puzzled.

"Hello, girls," he said. "I just found this carton of butter on Buttons's bed. Don't you need this to make the pies?"

"Yes!" exclaimed Kirsty, giving him a delighted hug. "Thanks, Dad!"

Rachel rubbed the butter into the flour and then added a little water. Soon she had a ball of golden dough. She wrapped it in plastic wrap and put it in the fridge to chill.

"Should we add the secret ingredient to the pie filling now?" Kirsty suggested.

Rachel nodded eagerly.

"It's an old family secret," she said with a smile. "Our own kind of magic!"

Kirsty picked up the jar of cinnamon and tried to unscrew the lid.

"Oh!" she said in surprise. "It's stuck! I must have tightened it too much when I put it back on earlier."

Rachel tried to open the jar, but it wouldn't budge.

"Let's ask my dad," she said. "He's really strong."

They hurried to the living room. Their parents were playing cards and listening to carols on the radio.

"Dad, can you undo this?" asked Rachel, holding out the spice jar. "We think Kirsty tightened it too much earlier."

Mr. Walker had to use all his strength to open the jar. At last, it popped open and he handed it back to Rachel.

"You must be stronger than you look, Kirsty!" he said with a laugh.

The girls hurried back to the kitchen, eager to add the secret ingredient. But when they reached the doorway, they stopped in amazement.

"What happened?" Kirsty cried.

All the drawers and cupboards were open and there was flour all over the kitchen. The dough was sitting on the kitchen counter, and it was covered in dirty fingerprints!

Suddenly, Rachel saw the top of a green head poking up from behind the kitchen counter.

"Look!" she exclaimed. "It's a goblin!"

Kirsty gasped. "What is he doing here?"

RAINBOW magic™

Which Magical Fairies Have You Met?

- ❑ The Rainbow Fairies
- ❑ The Weather Fairies
- ❑ The Jewel Fairies
- ❑ The Pet Fairies
- ❑ The Dance Fairies
- ❑ The Music Fairies
- ❑ The Sports Fairies
- ❑ The Party Fairies
- ❑ The Ocean Fairies
- ❑ The Night Fairies
- ❑ The Magical Animal Fairies
- ❑ The Princess Fairies
- ❑ The Superstar Fairies
- ❑ The Fashion Fairies
- ❑ The Sugar & Spice Fairies

SCHOLASTIC

Find all of your favorite fairy friends at
scholastic.com/rainbowmagic

RMFAIRY9